My Friend Is Sad

To my friend Marcia

ISBN-13: 978-0-545-07147-5
ISBN-10: 0-545-07147-X

38 17/0

Printed in the U.S.A. 40

First Scholastic printing, January 2008

My Friend Is Sad

By Mo Willems

An ELEPHANT & PIGGIE Book

SCHOLASTIC INC.
New York Toronto London Auckland Sydney
Mexico City New Delhi Hong Kong Buenos Aires

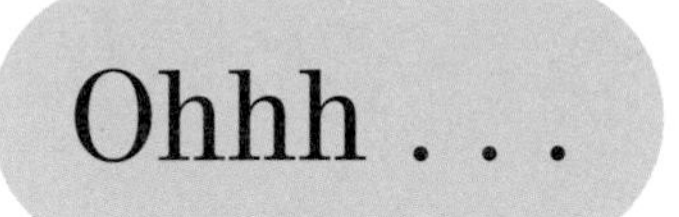
Ohhh . . .

My friend is sad.

I will make him happy!

Yee-haw!

A cowboy!

Ohhh . . .

Gerald loves cowboys.
But he is still sad.

A clown!

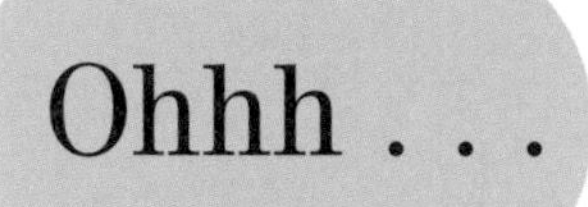
Ohhh . . .

Clowns are funny.
But he is still sad.

A robot!

How can anyone be sad around a robot!?

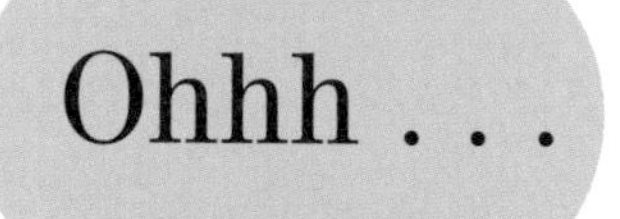

Gerald.
Piggie!

I am sorry. I wanted
to make you happy.
But you are still sad.

I am not sad now.
I am happy!

You are happy?

I am happy because you are here!

But I was so sad, Piggie.
So very SAD!

I saw a
COWBOY!

But you love cowboys!

I do.
I love cowboys.

But you were not there to see him!

Well, in fact, I . . .

THERE
WAS
MORE!

Then I saw a clown!

A funny,
funny clown!

But you were not there to see him!

But. . .

THERE WAS MORE!

I saw a ROBOT!

A COOL,
COOL ROBOT!

And my best friend
was not there
to see it with me.

But. . .
Um. . .
You see. . .

I am here NOW!

You are!
You are here now!

My friend is here now!

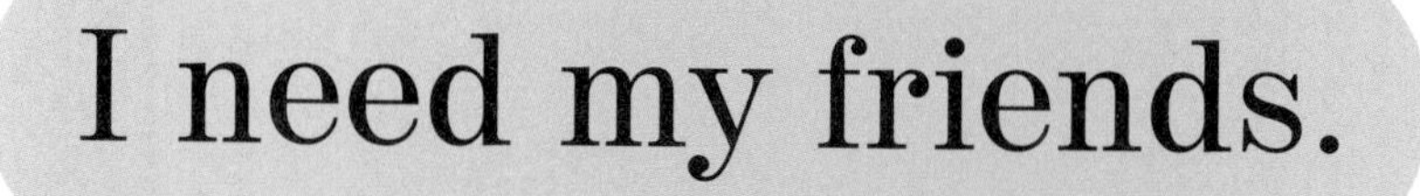
I need my friends.

You need new glasses. . . .